Noisy Neighbours

GERALDINE McCAUGHREAN

Illustrated by Mike Phillips

OXFORD
UNIVERSITY PRESS

OXFORD
UNIVERSITY PRESS

Great Clarendon Street, Oxford OX2 6DP

Oxford University Press is a department of the University of Oxford.
It furthers the University's objective of excellence in research, scholarship,
and education by publishing worldwide in

Oxford   New York

Auckland   Cape Town   Dar es Salaam   Hong Kong   Karachi
Kuala Lumpur   Madrid   Melbourne   Mexico City   Nairobi
New Delhi   Shanghai   Taipei   Toronto

With offices in

Argentina   Austria   Brazil   Chile   Czech Republic   France   Greece
Guatemala   Hungary   Italy   Japan   Poland   Portugal   Singapore
South Korea   Switzerland   Thailand   Turkey   Ukraine   Vietnam

Oxford is a registered trade mark of Oxford University Press
in the UK and in certain other countries

Text © Geraldine McCaughrean 2006

British Library Cataloguing in Publication Data
Data available

ISBN-13: 978-0-19-911340-8
ISBN-10: 0-19-911340-8

3 5 7 9 10 8 6 4 2

Available in packs
Stage 9 Pack of 6:
ISBN-13: 978-0-19-911333-0; ISBN-10: 0-19-911333-5
Stage 9 Class Pack:
ISBN-13: 978-0-19-911334-7; ISBN-10: 0-19-9171334-3
Guided Reading Cards also available:
ISBN-13: 978-0-19-911341-5; ISBN-10: 0-19-911341-6

Cover artwork by Mike Phillips

Printed in China by Imago

for Freddie

1

Mr Flinch

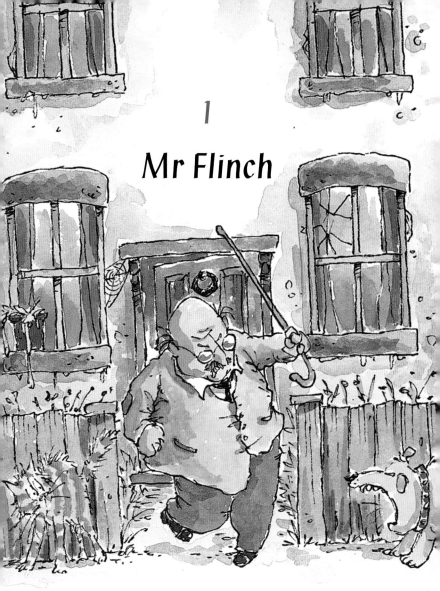

In a grim, grey house in a grim, grey
town lived an unhappy man.

It was not his grey house that
made Mr Flinch unhappy. It was not
that he was poor, because he was not.
Mr Flinch was a miser. He never gave
away a penny. (He never gave away
a smile either.) He was a mean
and miserable man.

Mr Flinch was miserable because of his neighbours.

On one side of Mr Flinch's grim, grey house stood a jolly red one. It belonged to Carl Clutch who mended cars.

Carl loved cars – and motorbikes
and vans and lorries. Every morning,
Mr Flinch woke up to hear hammers
banging, spanners clanging and
engines revving. The whole street
shook with the noise.

On the other side, in a bright blue
house, lived a music teacher called
Poppy Plink. Each morning, Poppy sat
down and played grand tunes on her
grand piano. After breakfast,
her students started to arrive.

Violins screeched, drums thundered and bassoons bellowed. Mr Flinch shut his window, but the noise still came through the wall. *Brum-brum, tootle-toot, bang!* His whole house shook and shivered.

He put his fingers in his ears.

He rapped on the wall... but his neighbours did not hear.

They were far too happy. They were mending cars and making music, and they loved their work.

Brum-brum, tootle-toot, bang!

Mr Flinch *rap rapped* until he made holes in his wallpaper. It did no good.

Mr Flinch locked himself in a cupboard. He wound old towels round his head.

He wrote angry letters, but tore them all up. 'Stamps cost far too much money!' he said.

Even in bed, he wore a hat to keep out the noise.

But the cars still revved and the music still jangled.

Mr Flinch was the grey filling in a noise sandwich.

'This can't go on,' Flinch thought to himself. He even shouted it out loud:

2

Nasty Tricks

Mr Flinch went next door to Carl's house. Carl was mending cars. It was easy to sneak into his kitchen and put a dead rat in the fridge.

'That will get rid of *him!*' said Flinch, and smiled a nasty smile. 'Nobody wants to live in a house with rats!'

At midnight, Mr Flinch climbed on to his roof and – carefully, carefully – crawled across the tiles. He put his head down Poppy's chimney and gave a long, loud, 'Hooowooowoooo!'

'That will get rid of *her*,' he said with a grim grin. 'Nobody wants to live in a house with ghosts!'

Then he climbed back into bed.

Next morning, Mr Flinch woke to a HUGE noise. Cars and lorries were stopping outside. He looked out of his window.

Carl was sitting outside in the road, with a table, a kettle, a loaf of bread and a bottle of tomato sauce.

Carl called to Mr Flinch, 'Can't use my kitchen today! Rats, urgh! My mum is cleaning up. She told me to eat my breakfast outside. That's how I got this great idea! Take-away breakfast! Drivers can stop here and buy breakfast.'

Just then, Poppy Plink came running
out of her blue front door. 'Oh, Mr
Flinch! Oh, Carl! Guess what happened
last night!'

'I give up,' said Mr Flinch, with a
smug smirk. 'Do tell.'

Poppy beamed with joy. 'Last night, angels sang down my chimney! They did, I promise!' She frowned. 'But the music wasn't very good! I think they want some new songs to sing! I'm sure they want *me* to write them, and I shall! Oh, I shall!'

She did.

Poppy still had to teach music
all day.

But at night she wrote angel music.
She made it nice and loud, with lots of
cymbals and trumpets.

It was all too much for Mr Flinch.

3

Mr Flinch has a Plan

Mr Flinch went next door to Carl's house.

He showed Carl a fistful of money. 'The day you move house, all this is yours!' he said.

'Anything you say, chief,' said Carl, wiping his dirty hands on a rag.

'As long as I can mend cars, I'll be happy anywhere.' Carl went on,
'I'll move out as soon as I can sell the house!'

Next, Mr Flinch went to Poppy's house and offered her a hatful of money. 'The day you move house, all this is yours!' he said.

'Of course! If that is what you want, dear heart!' cried Poppy.

She had never seen so much money in her life. 'As long as I have my music, I can be happy anywhere! I will move out just as soon as I can sell my little house!'

Mr Flinch went home a happy man
– well, as happy as a man like Mr
Flinch can ever be.

He felt in his empty pockets and
gulped. 'All that money gone! Ah, but
soon those noisy neighbours will be
gone, too!'

In a few days, Mr Flinch's
neighbours had sold up their houses.

Now, at last, he would have peace
and quiet – nothing but the noise of
mice scratching in the empty cellar.

4
Moving Day

Mr Flinch watched as Poppy Plink moved out. *Bo-jangle* went the piano as she pushed and bumped it down the steps.

'Going already are you, you pest?' he muttered. 'I pity the person who has to live next door to *you!*'

Seeing him, Poppy waved up at the window.

'Such luck, Mr Flinch!' she called. 'Fancy! A few days ago, I met someone who wants to move house too! We agreed to swap houses!'

Just then, Carl came out of his front
door carrying two heavy tool boxes.
He saw Poppy struggling with a harp
and went to help her. 'All set, Poppy?'
he said.

'All set, Carl! Isn't this fun!' she
replied.

Then Carl moved into Poppy's
bright blue house and Poppy moved
into Carl's jolly red one.

They helped each other to carry the
big things, like tables and sofas.

There's no

Then Carl had a house-warming party. He and Poppy sang, because they were so happy: 'There's no place like home!'

Mr Flinch heard it right through the wall of his house... even inside his cupboard, even with a towel round his head.

About the author

This was a Chinese folk tale. It made me laugh, so I retold it as if it were happening here and now (you can take a good story anywhere!).

To tell you the truth, I have a lot of sympathy with grumpy Mr Flinch. Noisy lawnmowers, car alarms, motorbikes and 'boom-boxes' make me grumpy too. However, neighbours are more important than a quiet life, and so I'm afraid Mr Flinch *IS* the villain.